MOUNTAIN MAN

BY

ROBERT E. HOWARD

British Library Cataloguing-in-Publication Data
A catalogue record for this book is available from the
British Library

Robert E. Howard

Robert Ervin Howard was born in Peaster, Texas in 1906. During his youth, his family moved between a variety of Texan boomtowns, and Howard – a bookish and somewhat introverted child – was steeped in the violent myths and legends of the Old South. Although he loved reading and learning, Howard developed a distinctly Texan, hardboiled outlook on the world. He became a passionate fan of boxing, taking it up at an amateur level, and from the age of nine began to write adventure tales of semi-historical bloodshed. In 1919, when Howard was thirteen, his family moved to the Central Texas hamlet of Cross Plains, where he would stay for the rest of his life.

At fifteen Howard began to read the pulp magazines of the day, and to write more seriously. The December 1922 issue of his high school newspaper featured two of his stories, 'Golden Hope Christmas' and 'West is West'. In 1924 he sold his first piece – a short caveman tale titled 'Spear and Fang' – for $16 to the not-yet-famous *Weird Tales* magazine. He published with the magazine regularly over the next few years. 1929 was a breakout year for Howard, in that the 23-year-old writer began to sell to other magazines, such as *Ghost Stories* and *Argosy,* both of whom had previously sent him hundreds of rejection slips. In 1930, he began a correspondence with weird fiction master H. P. Lovecraft which ran up to his death six years later, and is regarded as one of the great correspondence cycles in all of fantasy literature.

It was partly due to Lovecraft's encouragement that Howard created his most famous character, Conan the Cimmerian. Conan – a barbarian-turned-King during the Hyborian Age, a mythical period of some 12,000 years ago – featured in seventeen *Weird Tales* stories between 1933 and 1936, and is now regarded as having spawned the 'sword and sorcery' genre, making Howard's influence on fantasy literature comparable to that of J. R. R. Tolkien's. The Conan stories have since been adapted many times, most famously in the series of films starring Arnold Schwarzenegger.

Howard was enjoying an all-time high in sales by the beginning of 1936, but he was also deeply upset by the ill health of his mother, who had fallen into a coma. On the morning of June 11, 1936, he asked an attending nurse whether she would ever recover, and the nurse replied negatively. Howard walked to his car, parked outside the family home in Cross Plains, and shot himself. He died eight hours later, aged just thirty.

I was robbing a bee tree, when I heard my old man calling: "Breckinridge! Oh, Breckinridge! Where air you? I see you now. You don't need to climb that tree. I ain't goin' to larrup you."

He come up, and said: "Breckinridge, ain't that a bee settin' on yore ear?"

I reached up, and sure enough, it was. Come to think about it, I had felt kind of like something was stinging me somewhere.

"I swar, Breckinridge," said pap, "I never seen a hide like your'n. Listen to me: old Buffalo Rogers is back from Tomahawk, and the postmaster there said they was a letter for me, from Mississippi. He wouldn't give it to nobody but me or some of my folks. I dunno who'd be writin' me from Mississippi; last time I was there, was when I was fightin' the Yankees. But anyway, that letter is got to be got. Me and yore maw has decided you're to go git it. Yuh hear me, Breckinridge?"

"Clean to Tomahawk?" I said. "Gee whiz, pap!"

"Well," he said, combing his beard with his fingers, "yo're growed in size, if not in years. It's time you seen somethin' of the world. You ain't never been more'n thirty miles away from the cabin you was born in. Yore brother John ain't able to go on account of that ba'r he tangled with, and Bill is busy skinnin' the ba'r. You been to whar the trail passes, goin' to

3

Tomahawk. All you got to do is foller it and turn to the right where it forks. The left goes on to Perdition."

Well, I was all eager to see the world, and the next morning I was off, dressed in new buckskins and riding my mule Alexander. Pap rode with me a few miles and give me advice.

"Be keerful how you spend that dollar I give you," he said. "Don't gamble. Drink in reason; half a gallon of corn juice is enough for any man. Don't be techy--but don't forgit that yore pap was once the rough-and-tumble champeen of Gonzales County, Texas. And whilst yo're feelin' for the other feller's eye, don't be keerless and let him chaw yore ear off. And don't resist no officer."

"What's them, pap?" I inquired.

"Down in the settlements," he explained, "they has men which their job is to keep the peace. I don't take no stock in law myself, but them city folks is different from us. You do what they says, and if they says give up yore gun, why, you up and do it!"

I was shocked, and meditated awhile, and then says: "How can I tell which is them?"

"They'll have a silver star on their shirt," he says, so I said I'd do like he told me. He reined around and went back up the mountains, and I rode on down the path.

WELL, I CAMPED THAT NIGHT where the path come out on to the main trail, and the next morning I rode on down the trail, feeling like I was a long way from home. I hadn't went far till I passed a stream, and decided I'd take a bath. So I tied Alexander to a tree, and hung my buckskins near by, but I took my gun belt with my old cap-and-ball .44 and hung it on a limb reaching out over the water. There was thick bushes all around the hole.

Well, I div deep, and as I come up, I had a feeling like somebody had hit me over the head with a club. I looked up, and there was a feller holding on to a limb with one hand and leaning out over the water with a club in the other hand.

He yelled and swung at me again, but I div, and he missed, and I come up right under the limb where my gun hung. I reached up and grabbed it and let bam at him just as he dived into the bushes, and he let out a squall and grabbed the seat of his pants. Next minute I heard a horse running, and glimpsed him tearing away through the brush on a pinto mustang, setting his horse like it was a red-hot stove, and dern him, he had my clothes in one hand! I was so upsot by this that I missed him clean, and jumping out, I charged through the bushes and saplings, but he was already out of sight. I knowed it was one of them derned renegades which hid up in the hills and snuck down to steal, and I wasn't afraid none. But what a fix I was in! He'd even stole my moccasins.

I couldn't go home, in that shape, without the letter, and admit I missed a robber twice. Pap would larrup the tar out of me. And if I went on, what if I met some women, in the valley settlements? I don't reckon they was ever a youngster half as bashful as what I was in them days. Cold sweat bust out all over me. At last, in desperation, I buckled my belt on and started down the trail toward Tomahawk. I was desperate enough to commit murder to get me some pants.

I was glad the Indian didn't steal Alexander, but the going was so rough I had to walk and lead him, because I kept to the brush alongside the trail. He had a tough time getting through the bushes, and the thorns scratched him so he hollered, and ever' now and then I had to lift him over jagged rocks. It was tough on Alexander, but I was too bashful to travel in the open trail without no clothes on.

AFTER I'D GONE MAYBE a mile I heard somebody in the trail ahead of me, and peeking through the bushes, I seen a most peculiar sight. It was a man on foot, going the same direction as me, and he had on what I instinctively guessed was city clothes. They wasn't buckskin, and was very beautiful, with big checks and stripes all over them. He had on a round hat with a narrow brim, and shoes like I hadn't never seen before, being neither boots nor moccasins. He was dusty, and he cussed as he limped along. Ahead of him I seen the trail made a horseshoe bend, so I cut straight across and got ahead of him, and as he come along, I stepped out of the brush and threw down on him with my cap-and-ball.

He throwed up his hands and hollered: "Don't shoot!"

"I don't want to, mister," I said, "but I got to have clothes!"

He shook his head like he couldn't believe I was so, and he said: "You ain't the color of a Injun, but--what kind of people live in these hills, anyway?"

"Most of 'em's Democrats," I said, "but I got no time to talk politics. You climb out of them clothes."

"My God!" he wailed. "My horse threw me off and ran away, and I've been walkin' for hours, expecting to get scalped by Injuns any minute, and now a naked lunatic on a mule demands my clothes! It's too much!"

"I can't argy, mister," I said; "somebody may come up the trail any minute. Hustle!" So saying I shot his hat off to encourage him.

He give a howl and shucked his duds in a hurry.

"My underclothes, too?" he demanded, shivering though it was very hot.

"Is that what them things is?" I demanded, shocked. "I never heard of a man wearin' such womanish things. The country is goin' to the dogs, just like pap says. You better get goin'. Take my mule. When I get to where I can get some regular clothes, we'll swap back."

He clumb on to Alexander kind of dubious, and says to me, despairful: "Will you tell me one thing--how do I get to Tomahawk?"

"Take the next turn to the right," I said, "and--"

Just then Alexander turned his head and seen them underclothes on his back, and he give a loud and ringing bray and sot sail down the trail at full speed, with the stranger hanging on with both hands. Before they was out of sight they come to where the trail forked, and Alexander took the left instead of the right, and vanished amongst the ridges.

I put on the clothes, and they scratched my hide something fierce. I hadn't never wore nothing but buckskin. The coat split down the back, and the pants was too short, but the shoes was the worst; they pinched all over. I throwed away the socks, having never wore none, but put on what was left of the hat.

I went on down the trail, and took the right-hand fork, and in a mile or so I come out on a flat, and heard horses running. The next thing a mob of horsemen bust into view. One of 'em yelled: "There he is!" and they all come for me, full tilt. Instantly I decided that the stranger had got to Tomahawk, after all, and set a posse on to me for stealing his clothes.

SO I LEFT THE TRAIL AND took out across the sage grass and they all charged after me, yelling for me to stop. Well, them dern shoes pinched my feet so bad I couldn't hardly run, so after I had run five or six hundred yards, I perceived that the horses were beginning to gain on me. So I wheeled with my cap-and-ball in my hand, but I was going so fast, when I turned, them dern shoes slipped and I went over backwards into some cactus just as I pulled the trigger. So I only knocked the hat off of the first horseman. He yelled and pulled up his horse, right over me nearly, and as I drawed another bead on him, I seen he had a bright shiny star on his shirt. I dropped my gun and stuck up my hands.

They swarmed around me--cowboys, from their looks. The man with the star dismounted and picked up my gun and cussed.

"What did you lead us this chase through this heat and shoot at me for?" he demanded.

"I didn't know you was a officer," I said.

"Hell, McVey," said one of 'em, "you know how jumpy tenderfeet is. Likely he thought we was Santry's outlaws. Where's yore horse?"

"I ain't got none," I said.

"Got away from you, hey?" said McVey. "Well, climb up behind Kirby here, and let's get goin'."

To my astonishment, the sheriff stuck my gun back in the scabbard, and I clumb up behind Kirby, and away we went. Kirby kept telling me not to fall off, and it made me mad, but I said nothing. After a hour or so we come to a bunch of houses they said was Tomahawk. I got panicky

9

when I seen all them houses, and would have jumped down and run for the mountains, only I knowed they'd catch me, with them dern pinchy shoes on.

I hadn't never seen such houses before. They was made out of boards, mostly, and some was two stories high. To the northwest and west the hills riz up a few hundred yards from the backs of the houses, and on the other sides there was plains, with brush and timber on them.

"You boys ride into town and tell the folks that the shebangs starts soon," said McVey. "Me and Kirby and Richards will take him to the ring."

I COULD SEE PEOPLE milling around in the streets, and I never had no idee there was that many folks in the world. The sheriff and the other two fellows rode around the north end of the town and stopped at a old barn and told me to get off. So I did, and we went in and they had a kind of room fixed up in there with benches and a lot of towels and water buckets, and the sheriff said: "This ain't much of a dressin'-room, but it'll have to do. Us boys don't know much about this game, but we'll second as good as we can. One thing--the other fellow ain't got no manager or seconds neither. How do you feel?"

"Fine," I said, "but I'm kind of hungry."

"Go get him somethin', Richards," said the sheriff.

"I didn't think they ate just before a bout," said Richards.

10

"Aw, I reckon he knows what he's doin'," said McVey. "Gwan."

So Richards left, and the sheriff and Kirby walked around me like I was a prize bull, and felt my muscles, and the sheriff said: "By golly, if size means anything, our dough is as good as in our britches right now!"

My dollar was in my belt. I said I would pay for my keep, and they haw-hawed and slapped me on the back and said I was a great joker. Then Richards come back with a platter of grub, with a lot of men wearing boots and guns, and they stomped in and gawped at me, and McVey said, "Look him over, boys! Tomahawk stands or falls with him today!"

They started walking around me like him and Kirby done, and I was embarrassed and et three or four pounds of beef and a quart of mashed potaters, and a big hunk of white bread, and drunk about a gallon of water, because I was pretty thirsty. Then they all gaped like they was surprised about something, and one of 'em said: "How come he didn't arrive on the stagecoach yesterday?"

"Well," the sheriff said, "the driver told me he was so drunk they left him at Bisney, and come on with his luggage, which is over there in the corner. They got a horse and left it there with instructions for him to ride to Tomahawk as soon as he sobered up. Me and the boys got nervous today when he didn't show up, so we went out lookin' for him, and met him hoofin' it down the trail."

"I bet them Perdition hombres starts somethin'," said Kirby. "Ain't a one of 'em showed up yet. They're settin' over at Perdition soakin' up bad licker and broodin' on their wrongs. They shore wanted this show staged over there. They claimed that since Tomahawk was furnishin' one-half of the attraction, and Gunstock the other half, the razee ought to be throwed at Perdition."

"Nothin' to it," said McVey. "It laid between Tomahawk and Gunstock, and we throwed a coin and won it. If Perdition wants trouble, she can get it. Is the boys r'arin' to go?"

"Is they!" said Richards, "Every bar in Tomahawk is crowded with hombres full of licker and civic pride. They're bettin' their shirts, and they has been nine fights already. Everybody in Gunstock's here."

"Well, let's get goin'," said McVey, getting nervous. "The quicker it's over, the less blood there's likely to be spilt."

The first thing I knowed, they had laid hold of me and was pulling my clothes off, so it dawned on me that I must be under arrest for stealing the stranger's clothes. Kirby dug into the baggage which was in one corner of the stall, and dragged out a funny looking pair of pants; I know now they was white silk. I put 'em on because I hadn't nothing else to put on, and they fit me like my skin. Richards tied a

American flag around my waist, and they put some spiked shoes on my feet.

I LET 'EM DO LIKE THEY wanted to, remembering what pap said about not resisting an officer. Whilst so employed, I began to hear a noise outside, like a lot of people whooping and cheering. Pretty soon in come a skinny old gink with whiskers and two guns on, and he hollered: "Listen, Mac, dern it, a big shipment of gold is down there waitin' to be took off by the evenin' stage, and the whole blame town is deserted on account of this foolishness. Suppose Comanche Santry and his gang gets wind of it?"

"Well," said McVey, "I'll send Kirby here to help you guard it."

"You will like hell," said Kirby; "I'll resign as deputy first. I got every cent of my dough on this scrap, and I aim to see it."

"Well, send somebody!" said the old codger. "I got enough to do runnin' my store, and the stage stand, and the post office, without--"

He left, mumbling in his whiskers, and I said: "Who's that?"

"Aw," said Kirby, "that's old man Braxton that runs that store down at the other end of town, on the east side of the street. The post office is in there, too."

"I got to see him," I said, "there's a letter--"

Just then another man come surging in and hollered: "Hey, is your man ready? Everybody's gettin' impatient."

"All right," said McVey, throwing over me a thing he called a bathrobe. Him and Kirby and Richards picked up towels and buckets and we went out the opposite door from what we come in, and there was a big crowd of people there, and they whooped and shot off their pistols. I would have bolted back into the barn, only they grabbed me and said it was all right. We went through the crowd and I never seen so many boots and pistols in my life, and we come to a square pen made out of four posts set in the ground, and ropes stretched between. They called this a ring, and told me to get in it. I done so, and they had turf packed down so the ground was level as a floor and hard and solid. They told me to set down on a stool in one corner, and I did, and wrapped my robe around me like a Injun.

Then everybody yelled, and some men, from Gunstock, they said, clumb through the ropes on the other side. One of them was dressed like I was, and I never seen such a human. His ears looked like cabbages, his nose was flat, and his head was shaved. He set down in a opposite corner.

Then a fellow got up and waved his arms, and hollered: "Gents, you all know the occasion of this here suspicious event. Mr. Bat O'Tool, happenin' to pass through Gunstock, consented to fight anybody which would meet him. Tomahawk 'lowed to furnish that opposition, by sendin' all the way to Denver to procure the services of Mr. Bruiser McGoorty, formerly of San Francisco."

He pointed at me. Everybody cheered and shot off their pistols and I was embarrassed and bust out in a cold sweat.

"This fight," said the fellow, "will be fit accordin' to London Prize Ring Rules, same as in a champeenship go. Bare fists, round ends when one of 'em's knocked down or throwed down. Fight lasts till one or t'other ain't able to come up to the scratch at the call of time. I, Yucca Blaine, have been selected referee because, bein' from Chawed Ear, I got no prejudices either way. Are you all ready? Time!"

MCVEY HAULED ME OFF my stool and pulled off my bathrobe and pushed me out into the ring. I nearly died with embarrassment, but I seen the fellow they called O'Tool didn't have on more clothes than me. He approached and held out his hand, so I held out mine. We shook hands and then without no warning, he hit me an awful lick on the jaw with his left. It was like being kicked by a mule. The first part of me which hit the turf was the back of my head. O'Tool stalked back to his corner, and the Gunstock boys was dancing and hugging each other, and the Tomahawk fellows was growling in their whiskers and fumbling for guns and bowie knives.

McVey and his men rushed into the ring before I could get up and dragged me to my corner and began pouring water on me.

"Are you hurt much?" yelled McVey.

"How can a man's fist hurt anybody?" I asked. "I wouldn't have fell down, only it was so unexpected. I didn't know he was goin' to hit me. I never played no game like this before."

McVey dropped the towel he was beating me in the face with, and turned pale. "Ain't you Bruiser McGoorty of San Francisco?" he hollered.

"Naw," I said; "I'm Breckinridge Elkins, from up in the Humbolt mountains. I come here to get a letter for pap."

"But the stage driver described them clothes--" he begun wildly.

"A feller stole my clothes," I explained, "so I took some off'n a stranger. Maybe he was Mr. McGoorty."

"What's the matter?" asked Kirby, coming up with another bucket of water. "Time's about ready to be called."

"We're sunk!" bawled McVey. "This ain't McGoorty! This is a derned hill-billy which murdered McGoorty and stole his clothes."

"We're rooint!" exclaimed Richards, aghast. "Everybody's bet their dough without even seein' our man, they was that full of trust and civic pride. We can't call it off now. Tomahawk is rooint! What'll we do?"

"He's goin' to get in there and fight his derndest," said McVey, pulling his gun and jamming it into my back. "We'll hang him after the fight."

"But he can't box!" wailed Richards.

"No matter," said McVey; "the fair name of our town is at stake; Tomahawk promised to furnish a fighter to fight this fellow O'Tool, and--"

"Oh," I said, suddenly seeing light. "This here is a fight, ain't it?"

McVey give a low moan, and Kirby reached for his gun, but just then the referee hollered time, and I jumped up and run at O'Tool. If a fight was all they wanted, I was satisfied. All that talk about rules, and the yelling of the crowd had had me so confused I hadn't knowed what it was all about. I hit at O'Tool and he ducked and hit me in the belly and on the nose and in the eye and on the ear. The blood spurted, and the crowd yelled, and he looked dumbfounded and gritted between his teeth: "Are you human? Why don't you fall?"

I spit out a mouthful of blood and got my hands on him and started chewing his ear, and he squalled like a catamount. Yucca run in and tried to pull me loose, and I give him a slap under the ear and he turned a somersault into the ropes.

"Your man's fightin' foul!" he squalled, and Kirby said: "You're crazy! Do you see this gun? You holler 'foul' once more, and it'll go off!"

MEANWHILE O'TOOL HAD broke loose from me, and caved in his knuckles on my jaw, and I come for him again, because I was mad by this time. He gasped: "If you want to make an alley-fight out of it, all right! I wasn't raised in Five Points for nothing!" He then rammed his knee into my groin, and groped for my eye, but I got his thumb in my teeth and begun masticating it, and the way he howled was a caution.

By this time the crowd was crazy, and I throwed O'Tool and begun to stomp him, when somebody let bang at me from the crowd and the bullet cut my silk belt and my pants started to fall down.

I grabbed 'em with both hands, and O'Tool riz and rushed at me, bloody and bellering, and I didn't dare let go my pants to defend myself. So I whirled and bent over and lashed out backwards with my right heel like a mule, and I caught him under the chin. He done a cartwheel in the air, his head hit the turf, and he bounced on over and landed on his back with his knees hooked over the lower rope. There wasn't no question about him being out. The only question was, was he dead?

A great roar of "Foul" went up from the Gunstock men, and guns bristled all around the ring.

The Tomahawk men was cheering and yelling that I had won fair and square, and the Gunstock men was cussing and threatening me, when somebody hollered: "Leave it to the referee!"

"Sure," said Kirby, "He knows our man won fair, and if he don't say so, I'll blow his head off!"

"That's a lie!" bellered a man from Gunstock. "He knows it was a foul, and if he says it wasn't, I'll carve his liver with this here bowie knife!"

At these words Yucca keeled over in a dead faint, and then a clatter of hoofs sounded above the din, and out of the timber that hid the trail from the east, a gang of horsemen rode at a run. Everybody whirled and yelled: "Look out, here comes them Perdition illegitimates!"

Instantly a hundred guns covered them, and McVey demanded: "Come ye in peace or in war?"

"We come to unmask a fraud!" roared a big man with a red bandanner around his neck. "McGoorty, come forth!"

A familiar figger, now dressed in cowboy togs, pushed forward on my mule. "There he is!" this figger yelled, pointing at me. "That's the desperado which robbed me! Them's my tights he's got on!"

"What's this?" roared the crowd.

"A dern fake!" bellered the man with the red bandanner. "This here is Bruiser McGoorty!"

"Then who's he?" somebody bawled, pointing at me.

"My name's Breckinridge Elkins and I can lick any man here!" I roared, getting mad. I brandished my fists in defiance, but my britches started sliding down again, so I had to shut up and grab 'em.

"Aha!" the man with the red bandanner howled like a hyener. "He admits it! I dunno what the idee is, but these

Tomahawk polecats has double-crossed somebody! I trusts that you jackasses from Gunstock realizes the blackness and hellishness of their hearts! This man McGoorty rode into Perdition a few hours ago in his unmentionables, astraddle of that there mule, and told us how he'd been held up and robbed and put on the wrong road. You skunks was too proud to stage this fight in Perdition, but we ain't the men to see justice scorned with impunity! We brought McGoorty here to show you you was bein' gypped by Tomahawk! That man ain't no prize fighter; he's a highway robber!"

"These Tomahawk coyotes has framed us!" squalled a Gunstock man, going for his gun.

"You're a liar!" roared Richards, bending a .45 barrel over his head.

THE NEXT INSTANT GUNS was crashing, knives was gleaming, and men was yelling blue murder. The Gunstock braves turned frothing on the Tomahawk warriors, and the men from Perdition, yelping with glee, pulled their guns and begun fanning the crowd indiscriminately, which give back their fire. McGoorty give a howl and fell down on Alexander's neck, gripping around it with both arms, and Alexander departed in a cloud of dust and smoke.

I grabbed my gunbelt, which McVey had hung over the post in my corner, and I headed for cover, holding on to my britches whilst the bullets hummed around me as thick as bees. I wanted to take to the brush, but I remembered that blamed letter, so I headed for town. Behind me there rose a roar of banging guns and yelling men. Just as I got to the backs of the row of buildings which lined the street, I run into something soft head on. It was McGoorty, trying to escape on Alexander. He had hold of only one rein, and Alexander, evidently having circled one end of the town, was traveling in a circle and heading back where he started from.

I was going so fast I couldn't stop, and I run right over Alexander and all three of us went down in a heap. I jumped up, afraid Alexander was killed, but he scrambled up snorting and trembling, and then McGoorty weaved up, making funny noises. I poked my cap-and-ball into his belly.

"Off with them pants!" I yelped.

"My God!" he screamed. "Again? This is getting to be a habit!"

"Hustle!" I bellered. "You can have these scandals I got on now."

He shucked his britches, grabbed them tights and run like he was afeard I'd want his underwear too. I jerked on the pants, forked Alexander and headed for the south end of town. I kept behind the buildings, though the town seemed to be deserted, and purty soon I come to the store where Kirby had told me old man Braxton kept the post office. Guns was barking there, and across the street I seen men ducking in and out behind a old shack, and shooting.

21

I tied Alexander to a corner of the store and went in the back door. Up in the front part I seen old man Braxton kneeling behind some barrels with a .45-90, and he was shooting at the fellows in the shack across the street. Every now and then a slug would hum through the door and comb his whiskers, and he would cuss worse'n pap did that time he sot down in a bear trap.

I went up to him and tapped him on the shoulder and he give a squall and flopped over and let go bam! right in my face and singed off my eyebrows. And the fellows across the street hollered and started shooting at both of us.

I'd grabbed the barrel of his Winchester, and he was cussing and jerking at it with one hand and feeling in his boot for a knife with the other'n, and I said: "Mr. Braxton, if you ain't too busy, I wish you'd gimme that there letter which come for pap."

"Don't never come up behind me that way again!" he squalled. "I thought you was one of them dern outlaws! Look out! Duck, you fool!"

I let go his gun, and he took a shot at a head which was aiming around the shack, and the head let out a squall and disappeared.

"Who are them fellows?" I asked.

"Comanche Santry and his bunch, from up in the hills," snarled old man Braxton, jerking the lever of his Winchester. "They come after that gold. A hell of a sheriff McVey is;

never sent me nobody. And them fools over at the ring are makin' so much noise, they'll never hear the shootin' over here. Look out, here they come!"

SIX OR SEVEN MEN RUSHED out from behind the shack and ran across the street, shooting as they come. I seen I'd never get my letter as long as all this fighting was going on, so I unslung my old cap-and-ball and let bam! at them three times, and three of them outlaws fell across each other in the street, and the rest turned around and run back behind the shack.

"Good work, boy!" yelled old man Braxton. "If I ever--oh, Judas Iscariot, we're blowed up now!"

Something was pushed around the corner of the shack and come rolling down toward us, the shack being on higher ground than the store was. It was a keg, with a burning fuse which whirled as the keg revolved and looked like a wheel of fire.

"What's in that keg?" I asked.

"Blastin' powder!" screamed old man Braxton, scrambling up. "Run, you dern fool! It's comin' right into the door!"

He was so scared he forgot all about the fellows across the street, and one of 'em caught him in the thigh with a buffalo rifle, and he plunked down again, howling blue murder. I stepped over him to the door--that's when I got that slug in my hip--and the keg hit my legs and stopped, so I picked it up and heaved it back across the street. It hadn't no more'n hit the shack when bam! it exploded and the shack went up in smoke. When it stopped raining pieces of wood and metal, they wasn't any sign to show any outlaws had ever hid behind where that shack had been.

"I wouldn't believe it if I hadn't saw it," old man Braxton moaned faintly.

"Are you hurt bad, Mr. Braxton?" I asked.

"I'm dyin'," he groaned. "Plumb dyin'!"

"Well, before you die, Mr. Braxton," I said, "would you mind givin' me that there letter for pap?"

"What's yore pap's name?" he asked.

"Roarin' Bill Elkins," I said.

He wasn't hurt as bad as he thought. He reached up and got hold of a leather bag and fumbled in it and pulled out a envelope. "I remember tellin' old Buffalo Rogers I had a letter for Bill Elkins," he said, fingering it over. Then he said: "Hey, wait! This ain't for yore pap. My sight is gettin' bad. I read it wrong the first time. This is for Bill Elston that lives between here and Perdition."

I want to spike a rumor which says I tried to murder old man Braxton and tore his store down for spite. I've done told how he got his leg broke, and the rest was accidental. When I realized that I had went through all that embarrassment for nothing, I was so mad and disgusted I turned and run out of the back door, and I forgot to open the door and that's how it got tore off the hinges.

I then jumped on to Alexander and forgot to untie him from the store. I kicked him in the ribs, and he bolted and tore loose that corner of the building, and that's how come the roof to fall in. Old man Braxton inside was scared and started yelling bloody murder, and about that time a lot of men come up to investigate the explosion which had stopped the three-cornered battle between Perdition, Tomahawk and Gunstock, and they thought I was the cause of everything, and they all started shooting at me as I rode off.

Then was when I got that charge of buckshot in my back.

I went out of Tomahawk and up the hill trail so fast I bet me and Alexander looked like a streak. And I says to myself the next time pap gets a letter in the post office, he can come after it hisself, because it's evident that civilization ain't no place for a boy which ain't reached his full growth and strength.

www.ingramcontent.com/pod-product-compliance
Lightning Source LLC
Chambersburg PA
CBHW030137260626
47156CB00008B/2975